CANDY PLASTIC

JOANNA NADIN

illustrated by Sue Mason

WALKER
BOOKS

First published 2007 by Walker Books Ltd
87 Vauxhall Walk, London SE11 5HJ

2 4 6 8 10 9 7 5 3 1

Text © 2007 Joanna Nadin
Cover illustrations © 2007 Jason Ford
Interior illustrations © 2007 Sue Mason

This book has been typeset in StempelSchneidler

Printed and bound in Great Britain by Creative Print and Design
(Wales), Ebbw Vale

British Library Cataloguing in Publication Data:
a catalogue record for this book is available from the British Library

ISBN 978-1-4063-0422-0

www.walkerbooks.co.uk

SHE'S ...

A SUPERMODEL!

A SKI CHAMPION!

A SASSY HOLLYWOOD STAR!

SHE'S EVERY GIRL'S DREAM BIG SISTER!

SHE'S ...

CANDY PLASTIC

With moveable limbs, extendable hair
and a wardrobe to die for.*

*OUTFITS SOLD SEPARATELY.

WARNING: NOT SUITABLE FOR CHILDREN UNDER 5.

TOXIC IF EATEN.

GRIMCORP, INC.

DICK DANGER

'BEYOND THE CALL OF DUTY'

Join Dick Danger, the lantern-jawed,
iron-fisted, smooth-chested Special Forces
Agent, as he fights for freedom against
evil oppressors across the globe.

NO DICTATOR TOO SCARY!
NO MISSION TOO TOUGH!*

GRIMCORP, INC.

CAPTAIN FEARLESS

'FEARLESS BY NAME, FEARLESS BY NATURE!'

Captain Fearless, intergalactic superhero,

tirelessly saving the world from

the galaxy's most demonic monkey –

Voodoo Juju.

HE CAN LEAP HIGHER THAN A SKYSCRAPER!*

* USING JET BOOTS AND MINIATURE MODEL SKYSCRAPER –
NOT INCLUDED.

HE CAN WITHSTAND FIRE AND ICE!*

* WEARING PATENTED THERMO-SUPERSUIT – NOT INCLUDED.

HE CAN FLY!*

* USING ROCKET PACK AND WING ATTACHMENTS – NOT INCLUDED.

TOY OF THE YEAR 1999

GRIMCORP, INC.

ORGANIC EDIE

THE WORLD'S FIRST BIODEGRADABLE DOLL!

'IT'S WHAT'S ON THE INSIDE THAT COUNTS'

Handcrafted by indigenous tribes using fairtrade cotton, organic linseed and wool from free-range, extra-happy sheep.

DIRECT FROM MOTHER NATURE* TO YOU.

WARNING: MAY CONTAIN NUTS.

MAY GERMINATE ON CONTACT WITH WATER.

*A DIVISION OF GRIMCORP, INC.

THE EXPEDITION

Candy Plastic stamped across the floor of the doll's house in her red stilettos and flopped dramatically onto the sofa. "It's not fair!" she sobbed.

Organic Edie ignored her and carried on knitting. Candy, who did not like being ignored, tried again.

"Oh, it's too terrible!" she cried.

Edie clicked her needles noisily.

"Oh, well, if you're not going to ask I'll just have to tell you. Earlier today I heard the children's mother saying she's bought me a new outfit. But she's hidden it at the top of the playroom cupboard and I *so* want to find out what it is."

"Patience is a virtue, Candy," said Edie, laying down her knitting needles with a sigh.

"No, it's not, it's a very dull card game," snapped Candy. "And I have *nothing* to wear."

"Yes, you do. You have a wardrobe full of daft outfits."

"But I don't have this one," Candy said, sulking. "You don't understand. Just because you only have one shapeless, brown dress doesn't mean I should have to suffer too."

"I'm not suffering. And anyway, you could always lend me one of your dresses," said Edie brightly.

"As if!" Candy snorted. "Even if you did manage to squeeze into any of my clothes, you don't have the looks to carry them off. Anyway, if you won't help, I'm sure Dick will." And she flounced out of the doll's house and across the floor to the boys' side of the room, which, in contrast to the sparkles and sequins of the girls' side, was dark and gloomy and just a little bit smelly.

"Help, it hurts!" cried Captain Fearless, who was being held in a complicated arm-and-head lock by Dick Danger.

"Of course it hurts," said Dick. "You can't overpower an evil enemy without a bit of pain."

"But I'm not an evil enemy. I'm Captain Fearless!" wailed Captain Fearless.

"Hardly," snapped another voice.

The men looked up to see Candy standing there, tapping her pointy red toe in annoyance.

Dick dropped a grateful Captain Fearless from his stranglehold. "Just demonstrating my latest techniques, honey."

"Well, there's no time for that," said Candy. "I've got a mission for you."

"A mission, eh?" Dick rubbed his enormous jaw. "Then you've come to the right place. What is it? Bandits in the bathroom? A fearsome dictator banning TV and tight trousers?"

"Is it Voodoo Juju?" gasped Captain Fearless, who lived in permanent fear of his arch nemesis tracking him down.

"How many times?" said Candy. "Voodoo Juju doesn't exist. And even if he did – I mean, how scary can a monkey be? No, it's my new outfit, and it's stuck up there." She pointed to the top of the cupboard.

"Hmm, hardly worthy of the skills of a crack Special Forces Agent," said Dick.

Candy thought for a minute, which was quite a long time for her. But needs must when clothes were at stake.

"I think I saw a new weapon for you as well, Dick," she lied.

"Pur-lease," said Edie, who had come over to see what Candy was up to.

"Really?" asked Dick Danger, suddenly interested.

"Yes, a turbo-whatsit-thingummy."

"A Turbo-Charged Obliterator?" Dick asked excitedly.

"That's it. And new Superboots for Captain Fearless," she added.

"But you said they'd stopped making things for Fearless because he was too old," said Edie smugly.

"Yes, well, I..." stumbled Candy. "He must be making a comeback."

"I am?" gasped Captain Fearless.

"Yes. Now, come on, there's no time to waste. At this rate my new outfit will be out of fashion by the time we get there."

"Very well," said Dick. "This is the plan—"

"Hang on," said Candy. "Who put you in charge?"

"I'm always in charge," said Dick. "Don't sweat it, sweetie. Now, do you want this outfit or not?"

"Oooh, yes," said Candy, her eyes shining. "I wonder what I'll be this time. Maybe a ballerina ... or a brain surgeon. I look good in white."

"Just because you *look* like a brain surgeon doesn't mean you *are* one," said Edie.

"That's funny, because your outfit makes you *look* dull and boring and you *are* dull and boring," snapped Candy. "Everyone knows that looking the part is what really matters."

"Enough!" said Dick. "Let's get down to business. Right, men."

"And women," added Edie.

"And women," said Dick. "The plan is simple. Fearless, you will fly to the top of the cupboard and bring down the packages."

"F-f-fly?" stammered Captain Fearless. "B-b-but my rocket pack is broken and I've lost my snap-on wings."

"For heaven's sake," muttered Candy.

"Hmm. Luckily I have a Plan B," said Dick. "This is the ideal opportunity to try out my new Arrow Launcher. It's designed to catch fleeing enemy forces. You press this red button and the arrow shoots out and pierces the target. Then you wind this handle and it reels him back in."

"Hang on," said Candy. "I don't want holes in my new clothes."

"No need to fear, little lady," said Dick, lifting the Arrow Launcher into position. "I'm a crack shot. I'll aim for the packaging. Now everyone stand back!"

Everyone stood back.

"Ready?"

Everyone nodded.

"Aim – fire!" he shouted, and the arrow shot up towards the top of the cupboard. But halfway there it made a twanging noise, stopped, and hurtled back down to earth.

"Aaagh!" shrieked Candy. "It'll kill us all."

The toys ran for cover.

"Hmm. Not enough string," Dick muttered.

"If only Cowboy Tex were here," said Candy. "He could lasso it – he's the best cattle steer in ten counties, it says so on his box."

"Cowboy Tex," sneered Dick Danger. "He's useless in the face of modern combat. No – we just need to try Plan C."

"What's that?" asked Edie.

"Back to basics," said Dick. "We form a tower and then one of us climbs to the top."

"I'm scared of heights," said Captain Fearless.

"Then you can be the anchorman," said Dick, "with Edie on top of you."

"Who said I would be part of this?" said Edie.

"Oh come on, Edie," pleaded Candy. "I'll be your best friend."

"No, you won't."

"OK, I won't," admitted Candy. "But we can't reach it without you. You're an essential member of the team."

Edie thought for a minute. She was a firm believer in teamwork. "Oh, all right then," she said.

"Fine," said Dick. "So – Fearless at the bottom, then Edie, then Candy, and I'll climb to the top."

"Not likely," said Candy. "No one stands on me. It was my idea, so I get to climb up."

"It could be dangerous," warned Dick.

"Don't be silly," said Candy. "Anyway, you're too fat, you'd squash me."

"Fat? This is solid muscle," protested Dick, slapping his tummy. It boinged gently. "Well, of course, I don't see as much action as I used to," he said quickly.

"So it's decided," said Candy. "Come on then, everyone into position."

Captain Fearless braced himself as Edie climbed onto his shoulders.

"Are you sure about this, Dick?" he said. "What if I'm not strong enough?"

"That's defeatist talk. What are you? A man or a mouse?"

"Well, neither, really. I'm a sort of android, I suppose."

"Enough," barked Dick. "I'm coming up. Ninja-style."

"What's that?" asked Fearless. But before anyone could answer, Dick Danger leaped into the air, somersaulted and landed upside down on top of Edie.

"Ow!" she wailed. "My eye!"

"Sorry," said Dick. "Needs a bit of perfecting."

"Shall I get my nurse's outfit?" asked Candy.

"No!" said Edie quickly. "I'm fine, I'll sew it back on later."

"Right, then, here I come, ready or not," announced Candy, and she began to climb up the teetering tower.

"Aaagh, what's that?" yelped Captain Fearless.

"Ooops!" said Candy. "It's my stiletto. Maybe I should have worn my 'great outdoors' boots. They come with a torch and a pink sleeping bag."

"Come on," shouted Dick, from further up. "We can't hold on for that long."

"Keep your hair on," said Candy. "Oh, sorry – you army types don't have any, do you?"

"Candy!" warned Edie.

"I'm coming, I'm coming." Candy pulled herself up the stack, over Edie and her hanging-off eye, until she was face to face with the upside-down Dick Danger.

"Come on, Candy, you can do it," he said.

"I know I can," she snorted. "I don't need you to tell me."

"Hurry up," said Edie. "My shoulders hurt and I don't like having a mercenary balancing on my head."

"Mercenary?" said Dick. "I prefer 'soldier of fortune'."

"Same thing," sniffed Edie.

"All right, I get the picture," said Candy. She stuck her foot on Dick Danger's chin, took hold of his weapons belt, making sure not to grab a grenade by mistake, and pulled herself up.

"Oooh – I can see it!" she cried.

And she could, for there, on top of the cupboard, was a cardboard packet with the pink Candy Plastic trademark emblazoned across it.

"I can't quite see what's inside," said Candy.

"Are my Superboots there?" asked Captain Fearless excitedly.

"And my Turbo-Charged Obliterator? Can you see that?" asked Dick Danger.

"Ummm ... well ... actually ... no. Sorry!" said Candy. "But my outfit's definitely there, and that's the most important thing."

"Admit it, Candy, you knew all along you were the only one with a present, didn't you?" said Edie.

"Well..."

"Is that true?" demanded the upside-down Dick.

"I knew it!" said Fearless. "I'm doomed. I'll never have any superpowers again." And he began to cry. As he did, the tower began to wobble.

"Whoa!" said Candy. "Hang on. I haven't got it yet." She reached out until she was touching the edge of the packet. "Just a little bit further..."

Captain Fearless gave another enormous sob. The tower swung to the left.

"Aaaghhh!" everyone shrieked.

Then it swung to the right.

"Eeeek!" they wailed.

"Got it!" cried Candy triumphantly.

But at that very moment, Captain Fearless collapsed onto the floor in a gibbering heap. On top of him fell the almost-eyeless Edie, followed by Dick Danger and, clutching her prize, a jubilant Candy Plastic.

"My chest," groaned Dick. "I can't breathe."

"You've outdone yourself this time, Candy," said Edie, clambering out of the pile. "My eye's been torn off, you've winded Dick Danger and you've broken Captain Fearless's heart. I hope you're happy with yourself."

"I will be," said Candy smugly. "As soon as I get my new outfit on."

"What is it?" asked Edie. "A musical miniskirt? See-through roller boots?"

"No, it's a…" Candy held the packet out in front of her. "Oh!" Her face fell.

"What's wrong?" asked Edie.

"Um, nothing," said Candy, hurriedly hiding the package behind her back. "I think I'll save it for a special occasion."

"Come on," said Dick. "Don't be shy."

"Yes, come on," said Edie. "We're dying to see it. After all we've been through, it had better be worth it."

"But I—"

"Show us." Captain Fearless was unusually demanding.

"Show us!" they all chorused.

Hanging her shiny blond head in shame, Candy slowly held the package out so they could see.

Edie was the first to laugh, then Dick. Finally, even Captain Fearless joined in.

There, in Candy's hand, was a witch's outfit – complete with a pointed hat, a black cloak and a wart to stick on her nose.

"Ha ha ha. It was definitely worth it," chortled Dick.

"It'll really suit you," giggled Captain Fearless.

"You are what you wear," laughed Edie. "You said so yourself."

"Shut up!" protested Candy. "You're all horrible. I'll never wear it. It's awful."

"But you have to, Candy," said Edie.

"What do you mean?"

"If you don't wear it, the children's mother will think you don't like getting new outfits. She might never buy you anything ever again!"

"Really?" said Candy, shocked.

"Yes," said Edie. "Really. So you had better wear it all day."

And so she did. Candy wore the pointed hat, the black cloak and the wart until bedtime, and swore she'd never complain of having nothing to wear again.

Unless they brought out a new bubblegum-pink taffeta bikini. Now that, thought Candy, would really be worth it.

TREY PLASTIC

The playroom was asleep. The only sound was the gentle ticking of the pink Candy Plastic wall clock, counting down the minutes until—

"Aaaaaaagggggggghhhhhhhhhhhh!" came the shriek from the doll's house.

Edie rubbed her eyes and sat up in bed. What was that? she might have thought to herself had it not been obvious that the only answer could be "Candy Plastic". So instead Edie thought, What on earth is that ridiculous clothes horse up to now?

But she didn't have to wonder for long; Candy came running into Edie's room, wearing a silk dressing gown and fluffy slippers.

"Edie!" she wailed. "We're under attack. We're being ravished and ransacked! There's a *man* in my bedroom!"

"It's probably Dick Danger," said Edie, matter-of-factly. "He's always getting lost on night manoeuvres."

"It's not Dick. It can't be – he's not snoring and he smells nice."

"Captain Fearless?" suggested Edie.

"Wh–what?" stammered Captain Fearless, who had arrived with Dick Danger to see what all the commotion was about.

"Aaagh!" wailed Candy again.

"What's the matter, ladies?" asked Dick. "How can I be of service?"

"There appears to be a strange man in Candy's bedroom," said Edie.

"In my *bed* to be exact," said Candy.

"The fiend!" said Dick Danger. "Stand back, girls, I'm your man. I'm highly trained in dealing with damsels in distress."

"I am not a damsel, nor am I in distress," said Edie.

"Well I *am*," said Candy, "so get to it, sharpish."

Dick puffed out his enormous chest, jutted out his lantern jaw and, with his Super-Bazooka Gun in his hand, strode into Candy's bedroom.

The toys heard muffled voices, some oohing and huffing, and then Dick strode back again, a puzzled look on his face.

"Where is he?" wailed Candy. "Why have you left him there? Why haven't you tied him up, blindfolded him and tortured him until he tells all?"

"Um ... well..." started Dick.

"Well ... what?" asked Candy. "Don't tell me you've lost your nerve."

"Never!" protested Dick Danger. "It's just that he claims he's your husband, and says would I mind leaving him alone while he gets dressed."

38

"WHAT?" shouted Candy. "Me – married? And have a smelly, dirty man in the house? *Never!*"

"I think you are, actually," smirked Edie, pointing. "Look."

There, on the playroom floor, was an empty box.

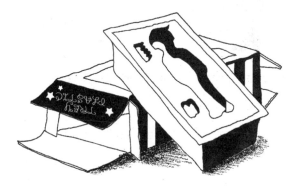

"His packaging!" gasped Captain Fearless.

"What does it say?" asked Dick Danger, who could smite enemies with one finger, but whose reading skills didn't go much beyond "the cat sat on the mat".

Candy looked in horror at the packet. "It says:

Meet the man in Candy Plastic's life!

HE CAN COOK!
HE CAN CLEAN!
HE CAN CHANGE A NAPPY!*
HE'S EVERY GIRL'S DREAM HUSBAND!
HE'S . . .

TREY PLASTIC

"Tray?" said Dick. "What kind of a name is that? It's not a name, it's something you put cups on."

But Candy had other matters on her mind.

"Baby?" she wailed. "When did I have a baby? Ugh! Horrible things. Pooing and crying all the time. It'll ruin my career." And she ran round the room frantically checking to see if there was any packaging for Bobby-Dee.

"What career?" asked Edie.

"Pick one. Supermodel, ski champion, celebrity chef. I'm all of them," snapped Candy, as she flung the cushions off the dolls' sofa.

"Well, look at it this way," said Edie. "On Trey's box it says he can change nappies, so you won't have to do that."

"She won't have to do that anyway," said a voice. "They haven't bought the baby … yet."

The toys swung round. There, in bright white trousers, a pink polo shirt and a glowing orange tan, stood Trey Plastic.

"*You!*" said Candy. "That's him. That's the imposter."

"I am *so* not an imposter!" said Trey, tossing his blond nylon hair so it whooshed and flicked fabulously.

"Oh no, not another one," groaned Edie.

"I'm your husband," announced Trey. "And I'm here to stay. Not that it's my choice. Your house is a pigsty."

Candy snorted in disbelief. "This can't be happening. I won't have it. Boys are just not allowed in the doll's house. There's nothing else for it. You'll have to go and live with Dick and Fearless."

Trey sized up Dick Danger. Dick Danger sized up Trey.

"And what do you do, soldier?" asked Trey.

"Just that, kid," drawled Dick Danger. "I'm a highly-trained, lantern-jawed, iron-fisted, smooth-chested, crack Special Forces Agent, saving the world from the forces of evil."

"I see," said Trey, smiling. "But, even so, I don't want to live on your side of the room. It smells."

"Does not," said Dick.

"Does too," replied Trey. "And you haven't even got a house. All you've got is a box, with bits of broken plastic in it."

"My Superboots and Defence Shield," said Captain Fearless sadly.

"Anyway, if you'll excuse me, I have things to do. The lighting is all wrong, the carpet needs hoovering and I have to make room in the wardrobe for all my fabulous outfits." And Trey swished back into the bedroom.

"Do something, Dick!" yelled Candy.

"I can't, he won't let me in until I clean all the

mud off my combat boots," Dick protested.

"But what if he's a spy for Voodoo Juju?" quailed Captain Fearless.

"Don't be silly," said Edie. "Even Voodoo Juju would be able to come up with a better spy than that."

"Something is wrong in the world of toys," said Dick, rubbing his chin. "A boy in the doll's house. The god is playing a trick on us."

"The god?" asked Candy.

"Yes, the all-powerful creator; the omnipotent Grimcorp, Inc."

"Grimcorp, Inc. is a person?"

"A god! He made us all."

"Not me," said Edie. "I'm made by Mother Nature."

"Who do you think made Mother Nature, sweetheart?" said Dick.

Edie looked horrified.

"Well, whatever," said Candy. "We have to get rid of him."

"Let's nuke him," said Dick.

"No!" protested Edie. "You warlords are all the same – you think guns and destruction are the answer to everything."

"We're not warlords, we're peacekeepers."

"Same weapons," Edie pointed out.

"But we use them for nicer reasons," said Dick.

"Well, what can we do?" Candy interrupted impatiently.

"Think what would annoy you most," said Edie. "You are married after all, so you must be fairly similar."

"Got it!" said Candy. "No one speak to him. There's nothing worse than no one looking at you or talking to you. He'll get bored and go somewhere else."

"Hmm, doesn't sound very menacing," said Dick. "But if it works, maybe I could include it in my list of special weapons."

"Come on, then," said Candy. "Let's go and ignore him."

So they did. Candy repainted her toenails, Edie knitted and Dick Danger practised torture techniques on Captain Fearless, who confessed his secrets immediately. He was terrified of loud voices, let alone having his hands stapled together. But after half an hour Edie ran out of wool and had to go back into the doll's house for more.

"Edie's going to ignore him right in front of his face," said Candy. "That'll show him."

But Edie didn't come back.

By lunchtime, everyone was wondering what Edie was up to, and why Trey still hadn't left.

"Let's go and check," said Candy.

"I thought we were meant to be ignoring him," said Captain Fearless.

But Candy ignored Captain Fearless instead and stomped into the bedroom to find out what was going on.

"Edie!" she gasped.

Edie was having her hair plaited by Trey.

"How could you?" sobbed Candy. "It's not like you even care about your hair anyway. You're always saying it's what's on the inside that counts."

"But a nice outside makes people take more notice of the inside," said Trey. "I think she looks marvellous. Doesn't it show off her cheekbones?"

"And it's so refreshing to meet someone who cares about their environment," said Edie.

"He only cares what colour it is!" snapped Candy. "And anyway, he's a boy! Boys are untidy and unclean and just, well, uggh."

"He's a lot neater than you are, Candy," said Edie, pointing to the dresses and shoes all over the floor and the lipstick smear on the mirror.

Candy pouted. "I might have guessed you would quit, you do-gooding, yoghurt-eating—"

"Sticks and stones," said Edie.

"Hmmmph," hmmmphed Candy, and stormed back out.

"Don't worry, sugarlips, we're still on your side," said Dick, after Candy had managed another hour of vigorous ignoring.

Candy looked up from her gossip magazine. Then she looked round.

"What do you mean 'we'? Where's Fearless?"

Dick got out his X-ray binoculars and surveyed the scene. Candy was right. Captain Fearless had disappeared.

"In the name of the free world, where is that intergalactic not-so-superhero?" demanded Dick.

"I'll tell you where!" whined Candy. "He's gone over to the *other side*. Listen."

Dick and Candy put their ears against the bedroom wall.

"She just doesn't seem to care," they heard Captain Fearless sob. "She keeps saying I'm not super at all. And Dick means well, but he's so busy protecting the world. No one really listens to me..."

"There, there, you poor thing, you," they heard Trey reply.

"That's it!" said Dick angrily. "I'm going to sort this out once and for all." And he marched into the bedroom, Candy close behind him.

"Now, just what do you think you're doing?" demanded Dick. "Brainwashing Captain Fearless. You know he's defenceless in the hands of the enemy."

"See?" said Captain Fearless. "Everyone thinks I'm rubbish."

"Oh, he doesn't mean it," said Trey. "He's just following orders, like a good soldier should." He turned to Dick Danger. "Say, do you work out? You have great muscle definition."

"Well ... I ... I do try to keep in shape, yes," admitted Dick, flattered. "You have to in my game."

"Dick – not you as well?" gasped Candy.

"But he's so … nice," said Dick.

Trey smiled at Candy, showing his perfect white teeth.

"Right, that's it. If he won't move out, I will," snapped Candy. "I'll be in my film-star trailer if you need me."

But no one did seem to need her. Candy sat in front of the mirror with its hundred light bulbs around the edge, and listened to the laughter coming from the doll's house. The trailer was not as glamorous as it had seemed when it first came out of its box. The sofa wasn't big enough to lie on, the lights went off when you closed the door, which was scary, and the wardrobe only had one dress in it – a very last-season peach frilly thing that Candy had never really liked. Besides, being on her own was boring. There was no one to gossip with, no one to talk to – or, rather, listen to her talk. She gasped in realization. She, Candy Plastic, was *lonely*! She actually *liked* having the other toys around. Well, she would just have to un-lonely herself. There was only one thing for it.

Candy waited until the others had gone to bed. Then, as softly as she could in her teetering heels, she crept back into the doll's house and into her bedroom.

"Who's there?" said Trey, turning on the light.

"It's me," said Candy. "Now listen up, Mr Plastic, here's the deal. You can stay. But only if you tidy up my clothes, do the cleaning and leave the gossip to me. Don't get any funny ideas about trying to kiss me either." And she kicked off her heels and got into bed.

"Oh, don't worry," said Trey. "You're *so* not my type, doll."

"Wait a minute – not your type?" said Candy. "How can I *not* be your type? I'm gorgeous. I'm a supermodel and an international show-jumper, my figure is perfect and I have thirty-seven pairs of shoes."

"Goodnight, Candy," said Trey.

Candy started to say something. But then she remembered how dark and cold and impossibly lonely the trailer had been.

"Goodnight, Trey," she said instead, and turned off the light.

THE RACE

"It's here, it's here," squealed Candy Plastic, running into the doll's house in a tight pink jumpsuit and goggles.

"What's here?" asked Edie with a sigh.

"And what *are* you wearing?" asked Trey. "That outfit is truly questionable."

"What do you mean, questionable?" demanded Candy. "It's my Formula Candy racing driver outfit. It's fabulous."

"But you don't have a car," said Edie.

"That's where you're wrong!" said Candy with delight. "My Plastic Fantastic Candymobile has arrived. Come and see!" And she ran outside.

The Candymobile really was fantastic. It was the exact colour of strawberry ice cream, with a silver lightning bolt on the bonnet.

"It's got a DVD player, a champagne-glass

holder, a magnifying make-up mirror so you can do your lipstick on the road and a flip-down hairdryer hood so you always look good on arrival."

"Nice touch," said Trey.

"I can't even begin to list the things that make it a potential death trap…" began Edie.

"So don't," said Candy. "You won't want a ride, then."

"I might, though," said Trey eagerly.

"What in the name of truth and justice is that?" demanded Dick Danger, who had finished his morning reconnaissance (which meant making Captain Fearless check behind the cupboard doors for the enemy) and was now primed and ready for action.

"It's my car," said Candy proudly. "Do you like it?"

"Car?" scoffed Dick. "That's not a car, it's a dodgem, a shopping trolley, a – dare I say it – a toy! Now, the Danger-Plane, that's a car!"

"I thought it was a plane," said Captain Fearless.

"It sounds like one," added Trey.

"Hah – I'm glad you noticed. It's actually a multi-functional Fully-Armed Regiment Transporter, or FART for short."

Captain Fearless giggled.

Dick ignored him. "It can travel via land, air or sea as long as you sellotape the glass lid shut. It's the fastest and toughest vehicle ever made."

"Well, mine has furry seat covers," said Candy. "Beat that."

"Mine has jet engines that glow red when you press a secret switch," said Dick.

"Mine has disco lights when you turn on the windscreen wipers."

"Mine has radar, a boot big enough to hold two enemy hostages and a button that makes a sinister beeping noise."

"You two!" said Trey. "There's only one way to settle this. A race!"

"A race?" said Candy.

"A race?" said Dick. "But the engine needs servicing and the beeping button is stuck in the 'on' position."

"I thought you said it was the fastest and toughest vehicle ever made!" said Edie.

"You'll need co-drivers," said Trey eagerly.

"I'll have Captain Fearless," said Dick quickly.

"Do I have to?" asked Fearless, who was scared of speed, and flying, and, well, most things, really.

"And I'll have Edie," said Candy, knowing full well that the doll would hate every minute of it.

"Hah!" said Dick. "Two women! You'll have no chance."

"Right, that's it," said Edie. "I won't have that sort of comment from you, Dick Danger. Show me to the Candymobile."

"What about me?" asked Trey, his face falling. "Can't I squeeze in somewhere?"

"No way," said Dick. "You'd be violating Special Forces procedure."

"You can be the judge," said Edie.

"Fine," said Trey huffily. "And the winner gets to wear my own specially designed Cape of Victory."

"Not likely," said Dick.

"No, it isn't, is it, because you won't be winning," Candy pointed out cattily.

"We'll see," replied Dick. "To the Danger-Plane!"

"To the Candymobile!" said Candy.

The contestants climbed into their vehicles and buckled up, or, in Candy's case, checked her eye shadow and switched on the musical air freshener.

"Here are the rules," said Trey, standing between the cars with a silk handkerchief in his hand. "You will do one circuit of the playroom. Whoever makes it back to the doll's house first wins. But there's to be no pushing, no use of weaponry and no other foul play."

"How dull," said Dick, revving his engine and glaring at Candy. Candy glared back and adjusted her driving goggles.

Trey raised his handkerchief. "Ready… Steady… GO!" He dropped it to the floor.

"Yee-hah!" yelled Dick Danger.

"Oooohhh!" squealed Candy.

"Heeelllp!" cried Captain Fearless.

"Tell me when it's over," wailed Edie,
shutting her eyes and gripping her seat.

The Danger-Plane sped off into the lead,
beeping ominously as it headed for the knight's
castle up ahead. But the Candymobile didn't
move.

"What's the matter?" said Edie, opening her eyes. "Why aren't we going anywhere?"

"Well, it's just that … I'm not sure how to start it," Candy admitted. "I thought it was this key here, but that just opens the bonnet to convert it into a picnic table."

"What about that knob?" asked Edie, pointing.

Candy twiddled it frantically. The DVD player came on.

"That's not it!" said Edie.

Then Candy tried a lever under the seat, but that just made the hairdryer hood flip down onto Edie's head.

"What on earth?" protested Edie. "Some car this is. Don't tell me this thing doesn't actually move."

But at that moment Candy pressed a small pink button on the dashboard and the Candymobile lurched into life.

"I knew I could do it," cried Candy. "I am a Formula Candy racing driver, after all. Let's go!" And with a crunch, she put her foot down and they zoomed off in hot pursuit of the Danger-Plane.

"Watch out for the
pick-up monkeys!" cried Trey
as Candy skidded round a corner,
narrowly avoiding a chair leg. "Oops, too
late." The car crunched across a plastic monkey.
Edie and Candy bumped into the air and back
onto their seats.

"Ow," they chorused.

"We've nearly caught them," cried Candy,
as they closed the gap on the Danger-Plane.

"Goddam those lady drivers," said Dick Danger,
checking his satellite tracking system. "I'm
going to have to use the jets."

"Ohhh noooo," wailed Captain Fearless, who had his hands over his eyes so he couldn't see how fast they were travelling.

Dick Danger pulled down hard on a lever marked "Warning – Danger-Jets". The bottom of the car lit up red and started to make a whizzy, whirring noise on top of the beeping, so that it sounded like a frenzied submarine.

"Help! It's broken.
It's going to blow up
and we're all going
to die!" wailed
Captain Fearless.

"Pah, it's fine," said Dick.

But it wasn't fine. All of a sudden the noisy
Danger-Plane zoomed out of control.

"Aaaaagh," shrieked Dick Danger and Captain

Fearless as they whizzed
straight up the ramp
of the play garage,
round the yellow spiral
driveway, out onto the roof and into mid-air.

"Where are you going?" shouted Trey from

below. "You're totally off course."

"Engage wings," cried
Dick, slamming his
fist on a red button
as they soared past
an incredulous Trey,

68

Candy and Edie. But no wings appeared. The Danger-Plane flew out the door and plummeted towards the stairs.

"It's not working, Fearless. We'll have to eject."

"E–e–eject?" stammered Captain Fearless.

"Five, four, three…" began Dick Danger.

"Nooooooo!" cried Captain Fearless.

"…two, one – GO!"

Dick pressed the eject button. He and Captain Fearless shot up into the air and straight towards the banisters.

"Aaaaaagggghhhhh," cried the pair as they followed the Danger-Plane over the edge of the landing. There was silence for a second, then—

Then silence once more.

"Oh my goodness!" cried Trey, clapping his hands to his cheeks.

"Crikey!" said Edie.

"Oops!" said Candy, and carried on driving.

"*Oops?*" repeated Edie. "It's more than oops."

"What do you care? You never liked Dick's guns and stuff, anyway," said Candy.

"Well, no," Edie admitted, "but I wouldn't wish harm on anyone. Stop the car. We have to help."

"Not likely," scoffed Candy. "We're in pole position. How do I look? Like a winner?"

"No, you look like a heartless, soulless, useless piece of plastic. Anyway, what does it matter what you look like? It's what's inside that counts."

"Poppycock. I'm a winner, he's a loser. I can't wait to see the look on his face—"

"Well, that's just it," said Edie angrily. "You might have to wait. Because if you don't help him now, he might not be around to see you win."

Candy pondered this awful thought. "Hmmm … all right." And she steered off course and onto the landing, with Trey running close behind them.

Candy couldn't find the Candymobile's brakes, so she simply switched off the engine and it came to a shuddering halt. Candy and Edie climbed out and, with Trey, peered over the edge of the landing. Lying at the bottom, in a heap of broken plastic, lay the Danger-Plane.

"It's too awful," sobbed Edie.

"My hero," cried Trey, wringing his hands. "Gone forever."

"Not quite," came a voice.

The toys looked down again.

"Dick!" gasped Trey. "You're alive!"

And he was. Just. In fact, he was clinging on to Captain Fearless, who, in turn, was dangling from the banisters by his Supercape, which had miraculously snagged on a leftover drawing pin.

"Quick, climb up!" cried Edie.

"I can't," said Dick. "Fearless is too slippery. Cursed Lycra."

"Sorry," said Captain Fearless.

"I'll get a skipping rope," said Trey. "We'll lower it down."

"No time," said Dick. "I'm slipping. It's all over."

"No, it's not," said Trey. "We just need something long. Think, everybody."

Everybody thought.

"I've got it!" cried Edie, and she turned to Candy. "Your hair."

"Excuse me?" said Candy, touching her blond tresses. "What about it?"

"It's extendable. We'll lower it down and Dick can climb up it."

"Are you mad?" gasped Candy. "I've just washed it. And anyway, it's too shiny, he'll never get a good hold."

"Yes, he will," said Trey. "If it's plaited."

"Brilliant," said Edie.

"Er, no," said Candy. "Plaits are *so* last year."

"You have to do it," cried Dick Danger, who was hanging on by one hand now.

Candy looked down at Dick. "Only if you admit defeat," she said.

"Never!" cried Dick. "Special Forces would rather die."

"OK, then," said Candy, and she started walking back to the Candymobile.

"Please!" wailed Fearless. "I don't think my Supercape will hold much longer and I'm scared of falling."

"Am I the best?" Candy asked Dick, hands on her hips.

"Mmmmghhh… Yes. All right. You are the best."

"Thank you," said Candy.

"Now, please, Candy Plastic, let down your hair!" wailed Captain Fearless.

"Very well."

"Thank goodness," said Trey.

Edie turned the key on Candy's neck. Her hair grew and Trey plaited it quickly. When it was ready they let it down to Dick, who grabbed hold of it and began to haul himself up.

"Ow!" said Candy. "Be careful. If I end up bald and ugly, I'll sue you."

"There's a thought," muttered Edie.

Dick carried on climbing until he had passed Captain Fearless and pulled himself through the banisters. Then he unsnagged Captain Fearless and pulled him up, too.

"Hurray!" cried Trey.

"Thanks, baby doll," said Dick to Candy, who was desperately trying to unplait her hair. "You're a winner in my book, any day."

Candy blushed. For the first time in her life, she realised that there were other ways of winning, after all.

Maybe Edie had been right all along. Maybe what you did *was* more important than how you looked.

"Do I get the Cape of Victory then?" Candy smiled at Trey.

"No," said Trey. "I think someone else needs it more than you." And he handed the purple velvet cloak to Captain Fearless.

"G–g–gosh. Thanks," stuttered the superhero.

"Your Supercape helped save Dick. Maybe you do have special powers after all," said Trey.

"Hah, not likely," said Candy. "He's just lucky it was made from such tough, old and – frankly – unattractive material."

"Candy!" warned Edie.

"Sorry," said Candy.

THE ESCAPE

"What *do* you think you look like?" asked Edie.

Candy Plastic, who was dressed in a black catsuit and shiny black boots, gave a little twirl.

"Do you like it?" she asked.

"What are you supposed to be?" asked Edie.

"Well, obviously, I'm an international spy. Look – this lipstick is actually a secret laser beam, I've got a digital voice recorder in my shoe and a hidden camera in my headband."

"Frankly, you look daft. But that's nothing new," said Edie.

"Well, you won't be so mean when I find out a super international secret, will you?"

Edie shook her head in disbelief and went back to her crocheting.

Annoyed, Candy decided to go and do some spying.

"I may be some time," she announced to no one in particular. "But do not fear, I have a stun gun hidden in my underwear."

"What is she on about?" asked Trey, who was busy dusting the hoover.

"Don't ask," said Edie.

Candy crept along the wall and then around the door onto the landing.

"Stop, sweet cheeks! There could be danger out there!" warned Dick Danger. "You need back-up."

"What if Voodoo Juju is hiding on the stairs?" said Captain Fearless.

Suddenly Candy ran back into the room, a look of horror on her face.

"You're all doomed," she panted.

"It's Voodoo Juju," cried Captain Fearless. "I knew it."

"No, it's not, it's worse," said Candy.

"What could possibly be worse than the galaxy's most demonic monkey?" wailed Captain Fearless.

"This," said Candy. "Listen up. I just heard the children's mother tell them they have until the end of the day to choose unwanted toys to go to poor orphan children. You're all in danger!"

"Oh, this is terrible," said Dick. "The outside world is full of evil dictators. I will be on a permanent mission."

"I need at least two days to pack my wardrobe!" cried Trey.

"Hang on a minute," said Edie. "What do you mean, '*You're* all doomed'? What about you?"

"Well obviously, they won't pick me. I'm Candy Plastic – supermodel, ski champion and sassy Hollywood star. Anyway, I was last in."

"No, you weren't, Trey was," Edie said.

"Well, I'm the most beautiful," boasted Candy, stamping her spy boot and tossing her hair.

"Well, I can save whole nations from warped madmen," said Dick. "What can you do?"

"I look good in yellow and, believe me, that's a real talent," said Candy. "Edie will go, of course, she's boring and fat."

"I'm not boring, I'm natural. And I think the phrase is 'anatomically correct'," said Edie angrily.

"There's nothing correct about legs that shapeless. And what's wrong with being man-made? Life without Lycra is no life at all."

"It'll be me," Captain Fearless shook his head sorrowfully. "It's all over. I've known this was coming for some time. No one wants an old-fashioned superhero like me. My cape is torn, my defence shield is broken and I'm frightened of fighting."

"Buck up, Fearless," said Dick. "That's defeatist talk."

"It's true, though," said Candy. "He's *so* last century, like Tamagotchis and 'Baby Wants a Wee Wee' dolls."

"What's a Tamagotchi?" asked Trey.

"Exactly," replied Candy.

"Look, no one's safe. Not even you, little lady," said Dick, pointing at Candy. "There's no knowing what those kids will decide. There's nothing else for it. We'll have to escape."

"E–e–escape?" stammered Captain Fearless.

"Yes," said Dick. "I, Dick Danger, lantern-jawed, iron-fisted, smooth-chested, crack Special Forces Agent, will lead you to freedom in the face of danger and destruction."

"How masterful," said Trey.

"The plan is simple. The front door is out of the question – too many chances of being seen. The back door is a no-go zone on account of the dog. We'll have to go out—" Dick paused for effect "—the window." And he pointed dramatically.

"But it's too dangerous," sobbed Captain Fearless.

"Nonsense," said Dick Danger. "We go past the pick-up monkeys, through the Sticklebricks – watch you don't slip, those prongs can be painful – over the train tracks, through the garage and into the knight's castle. Then, up to the turrets and, from there, I'll give you all a leg-up to the windowsill. Are you ready, troops?"

"Wait," cried Candy. "What shall I wear? I could be a Snowbunny, or maybe even a Spacegirl. What do you think?"

"There's no time for that," said Dick. "It's a come-as-you-are kind of mission. My favourite. Now go, go, GO!"

With only a minor setback when Captain Fearless accidentally set off the train set with Edie still on the tracks, the toys reached the windowsill and looked down at the garden below.

"Ugh," said Candy. "There's mud and stuff."

"Of course there is," said Dick. "It's dangerous terrain out there. Organic Edie – your main problem is going to be water."

"Oh no, I'll germinate," she gasped, clutching her tummy, which was stuffed with seeds.

"Not if you wear my chemical warfare suit," said Dick. "Here – nothing, not even Ribena, gets through this baby." He handed her a brown boiler suit from his backpack.

"What's it made of?" said Edie.

"Melted cow bones and rubber," said Dick.

Edie looked queasy.

"Listen, doll. A tough situation calls for tough choices. Live or die – you decide."

Edie put on the suit.

"Trey," continued Dick. "It's going to be rough out there. You may not see a dustpan for a while. Are you prepared?"

"I'd trust you with my life," said Trey bravely.

Dick turned to Captain Fearless. "I don't want to worry you, but somewhere out there Voodoo Juju is waiting. You could be playing straight into enemy hands."

"It's no use," sobbed Fearless. "Who am I kidding? I might as well stay and save the rest of you from danger."

Dick Danger looked meaningfully at the not-so-superhero. "No one gets left behind on my watch, soldier," he said, and clapped him on the shoulder.

"Hey, sweetcakes," he said, turning to Candy. "You're quiet. Are you ready to jump?" Candy nodded quickly and gave a weak smile.

"Right," said Dick. "Weapons – check! Sonar radar helmet – check! Sweets for innocent children – check! Hold hands, troops, we're going over the top. On the count of three – one…!"

Everyone held hands. Everyone except Candy.

"…Two…!"

"What are you doing, Candy?" Edie demanded.

"Nothing," said Candy. "I just don't want to hold hands."

"Come on," said Trey. "We have to go together."

"…Three!"

"Candy!"

But it was too late. Candy watched from the windowsill as the toys fell towards the garden.

"Aaaghh!" they cried as they landed in the grass with a *whump*! Dick was the first to get up. "Man down, man down!" he shouted.

"Girl up, actually," shouted Candy from above.

"But you're in danger," shouted Dick. "The enemy is closing in."

"I think not," said Candy. "I'm the best, most beautiful, most talented toy in the world. I'm Candy Plastic – who could possibly live without me?"

"You had better be sure," said Edie.

"What do you mean?" asked Candy.

"Well, now you're the only toy left, there's no one else for the children to choose but you, is there?"

"Oh," said Candy, suddenly feeling a bit sick. "I hadn't thought of that."

"Enjoy your new life with the orphans," continued Edie. "Of course, there'll be no more new outfits for you. They won't be able to afford them. You'll have to wear that stupid spy suit forever. And even if you do get to stay there'll be no one to play with, no one to gossip with, no one to admire you in your Santa's Little Helper outfit on Christmas day…"

Candy gasped. This was truly terrible. A life without admiration was no life at all. She had no choice…

"Look out," she cried. "I'm coming down!" And she closed her eyes and stepped into the void.

"Eeeeeeekkkk!" she screamed, as she tumbled head over heels through the air.

"Left a bit," instructed Dick Danger.

"How do I do that?" yelled Candy, still spinning.

"Watch out for the railings," added Edie helpfully.

"Go right, go right!" shouted Fearless.

"I can't … help … aagghh…"

There was an almighty splash. Candy had landed face down in a muddy puddle.

"Uggghh. Hgggllmph!" she spluttered, as she stood up. "Oh, yuck, yuck, yuck. This is all your fault," she said, turning to Edie. "I should never have listened to you." And she stamped her foot, which just made her wetter.

"Don't blame me if you don't look where you're going," said Edie.

"Troops!" shouted Dick. "Stop! The mission isn't over yet."

"What now?" asked Captain Fearless.

"We need to find out when the coast will be clear," replied Dick. "That could be days, or even weeks, away."

"No, it won't," said Edie. "The children had to choose the unwanted toys *today*."

"Hmm. You're right," admitted Dick. "OK – we need a brave volunteer to cross enemy lines and report back when it's safe to re-enter the zone. I'd go myself, of course, but I'm needed to lead manoeuvres."

"Me, me!" said Trey, eager to please. "I'll go."

"Don't be stupid," said Candy. "You're wearing white. They'll spot you immediately."

"Well, you're the only one dressed for espionage," Edie pointed out. "You go."

"Fine," said Candy. "I will. Even though I have no idea what espionage is, it's certainly true I am an international spy."

Candy shook out her hair, stepped out of the puddle and crept towards the cat flap in the back door. Carefully, she lifted it up a little and poked her boot through.

"What in the name of the free world are you doing?" demanded Dick.

"Ssshh," whispered Candy. "It's my digital voice recorder. I can hear them talking." She pressed a button on the boot, the heel opened and something started whirring.

"Cunning," said Dick, with barely concealed jealousy.

After a minute, Candy pulled out her boot and hopped back. "Listen," she said, and twisted the heel around. The recorder started to play. The voices were muffled. But everyone could hear exactly what the children's mother was saying.

"...and no dolls or action figures. Those poor children don't need that sort of toy. Find something educational, like Lego."

Candy stopped it and turned to face the other toys.

"So we're safe," said Captain Fearless.

"We were never *doomed* in the first place," said Edie. "I've been squished inside this hideous piece of dead animal and rubber for nothing and it's all your fault." She glared at Candy.

"False intelligence," said Dick Danger. "That's a serious crime."

"I don't know what you lot are annoyed about," said Candy. "Look at me. My nail varnish is chipped, my hair is a mess and there's something crawling up my spy suit."

"Well, I think it's marvellous," said Trey.

"You do?" asked Candy.

"Yes," said Trey. "We all stuck together. Even Candy – in the end. And that's the most important thing."

"We sure did," said Dick, and he turned to Candy Plastic. "You can be on my team any day, honey pie."

"You're one of us now," said Captain Fearless.

"I am?" said Candy. She looked at them all – the out-of-date and not very super Captain Fearless; Dick Danger, with his ridiculously large jaw and obsession with guns; Edie, who never cared how she looked; and Trey, whose biggest fear was that the hoover might break down. How could she – the amazing, the

beautiful, the fantastic Candy Plastic – belong
with this band of misfits? But then she looked
down at her muddy outfit and felt her ruined
hair-do and realized that, for once, she really
was one of them.

"You're right," she said. "Come on, team.
Let's get back to the playroom."

And how long did the nice Candy last? Just about as long as it took her to get back to the doll's house, redo her hair and put on her Olympic Ice-Dance Star leotard.

"Oh, I really am the best," she said as she gazed at her reflection in the mirror. But she said it quietly. So that not even Edie could hear. Because, just for a little while, being one of the gang was kind of nice.